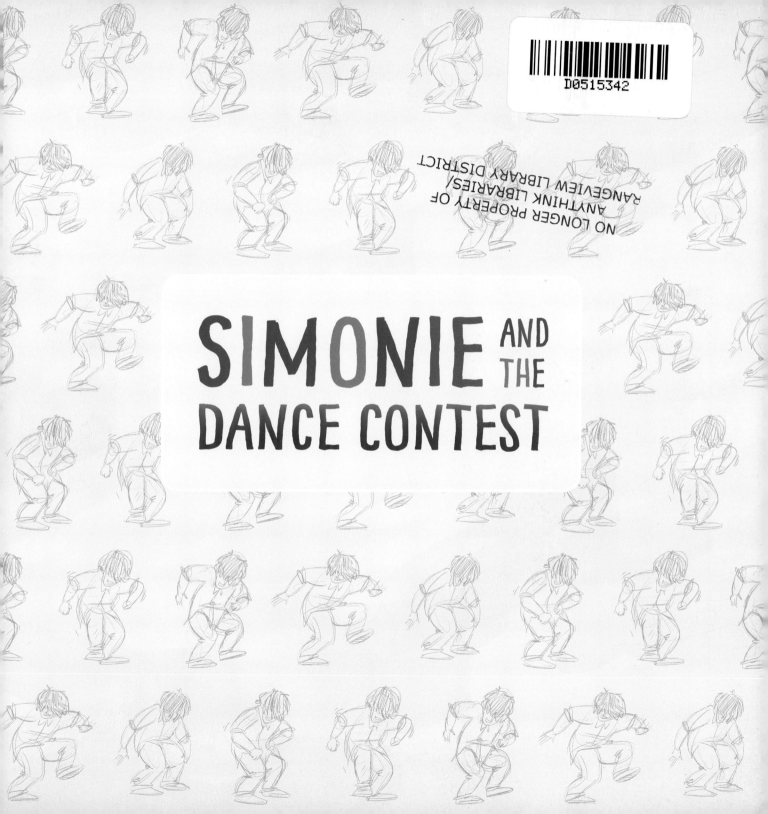

SIMONIE AND THE DANCE CONTEST

NO LONGER PROPERTY OF
ANYTHINK LIBRARIES/
RANGEVIEW LIBRARY DISTRICT

D0515342

This book is dedicated to the memory of my brother, Roger Peter Matthews, who loved to read and dance. When he wasn't travelling and working all over the world, he was making loving memories with his children and all those who knew and loved him. I would also like to dedicate this book to all children, especially my students in Taloyoak, Nunavut, who are experiencing the joy of learning to read and dance.

Published by Inhabit Media Inc. | www.inhabitmedia.com

Inhabit Media Inc. (Iqaluit) P.O. Box 11125, Iqaluit, Nunavut, X0A 1H0
(Toronto) 191 Eglinton Avenue East, Suite 310, Toronto, Ontario, M4P 1K1

Design and layout copyright © 2018 Inhabit Media Inc.
Text copyright © 2018 Inhabit Media Inc.
Illustrations by Ali Hinch copyright © 2018 Inhabit Media Inc.

Editors: Neil Christopher, Kathleen Keenan, and Grace Shaw
Art Director: Danny Christopher
Designers: Astrid Arijanto and Sam Tse

All rights reserved. The use of any part of this publication reproduced, transmitted in any form or by any means, electronic, mechanical, photocopying, recording, or otherwise, or stored in a retrievable system, without written consent of the publisher, is an infringement of copyright law.

We acknowledge the support of the Canada Council for the Arts for our publishing program.
This project was made possible in part by the Government of Canada.

Printed in Canada

ISBN: 978-1-77227-224-6

Library and Archives Canada Cataloguing in Publication

Matthews, Gail, 1954-, author
    Simonie and the dance contest / by Gail Matthews ; illustrated by Ali Hinch.

ISBN 978-1-77227-224-6 (softcover)

    I. Hinch, Ali, illustrator II. Title.

PS8626.A864S56 2018   jC813'.6   C2018-905231-7

SIMONIE AND THE DANCE CONTEST

BY GAIL MATTHEWS · ILLUSTRATED BY ALI HINCH

Simonie loved to read. He loved it so much that he practised reading syllabics everywhere he went with *Anaana*. He read signs in the stores, at the skating arena, and even at the health centre. One morning at the arena, they saw a poster that showed people dancing together.

"What does that say, Simonie?" asked Anaana.

Simonie walked right up to the poster so he could see the words clearly. "Christmas Jigging Dance Contest," he read. "December fourteenth. Anaana, it's the community dance contest!"

The only thing that Simonie loved more than reading was dancing. He loved going to the community dance, where he could dance with all his friends and neighbours. The contest would be just as much fun—maybe even more!

Simonie was so excited that he danced part of the way home, imagining himself stepping across the dance floor in front of all his friends.

When they got home, Simonie burst through the door. *Ataata*, who was making dinner, looked up, startled.

"Ataata, Ataata! This year I want to enter the jigging dance contest! Can you teach me some new steps? I have to practise!" Simonie said.

Ataata laughed and promised he would help Simonie prepare for the contest.

Over the next few weeks, Simonie practised and practised his dancing. He spun, he stepped, and he even tried hopping around like a hare. When he felt ready, he asked Ataata to watch him dance.

"That's good, Simonie," said Ataata. "But you have to feel the movements and the music. They go together."

Simonie wasn't sure what Ataata meant. He knew he was already listening to the beat of the music and dancing in time to it. How could he feel the music, too?

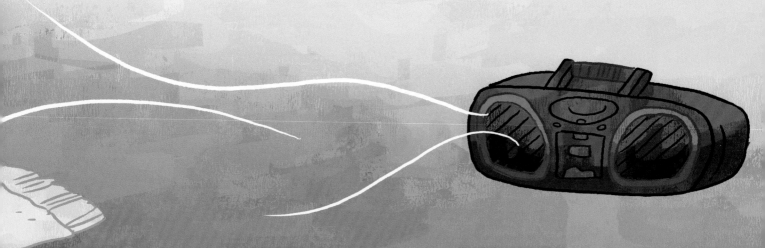

Simonie needed a partner. The next time he saw his friend Dana, he said, "I'm going to enter the dance contest. How about you?"

"Yes! Let's dance together," said Dana.

At morning recess, when the sun came up and gave them some light, Simonie and Dana practised on the playground. The snow was flat and crisp, so Simonie and Dana stamped out a circle and practised dancing in opposite directions inside it.

It was hard work! The more Simonie danced, the better he got. But something was missing. He still didn't understand how to feel the music, like Ataata had said.

After a few days of practising with Dana, Simonie saw his friend David at the arena.

Simonie knew that David was a good dancer. At last year's competition, he had drifted across the dance floor like cottongrass blown by a gust of wind. Simonie wondered if he was good enough to dance like David. Feeling nervous, he said he was entering the contest this year.

"That's so cool!" said David. "Let's practise together!"

Simonie grinned and nodded. He couldn't wait to get even better!

For the next few weeks, Simonie danced everywhere he could. He danced when he got out of bed in the morning. He and Dana danced together in the schoolyard. He danced while David sang or stomped a beat for him. But something was still missing.

When Simonie met David for their last practise together before the contest, Simonie remembered Ataata's words. "David, how do you dance so well?" he asked.

David smiled. "I just dance the way the music feels," he said.

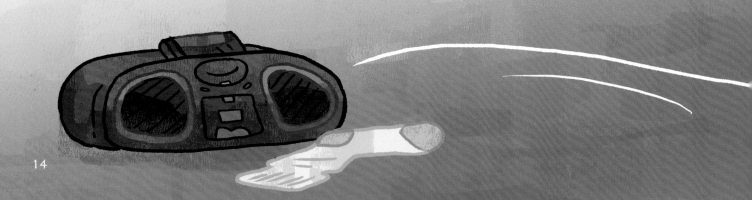

When Simonie got home, he thought about what David had said. He turned on the music, closed his eyes, and listened, concentrating on the music and nothing else. He felt his body begin to sway as it responded to the music. He felt alive. He felt like flying.

Simonie open his eyes, stood up, and danced like he'd never danced before.

As he walked to the community centre with Anaana and Ataata on the night of the contest, Simonie felt too nervous to dance. "What if I forget what to do?" he worried.

"I used to get nervous when I danced as a little girl," Anaana said, taking Simonie's hand. "Remember to enjoy the dance. Whatever's in your heart, express it!"

Inside the community centre, it was warm and bright, with Christmas decorations and lights shining all around. At the front, the musicians sat warming up their instruments.

Simonie saw some of his friends from school sitting in a big circle. His hands started to sweat from nervousness.

"Simonie!" said David, nudging him on the shoulder. "Are you ready?"

"I'm so nervous!" Simonie confessed. "Don't you get nervous before you dance?"

David smiled. "Just pretend we're practising!"

The musicians began to play, and the emcee called out the names. As their names were called, pairs of dancers came up and danced in opposite directions around the circle. People cheered and clapped their hands to the music.

Finally, Simonie and Dana were called. Simonie felt a sudden lurch in the pit of his stomach. He ignored it, and everyone watching, and walked out into the circle.

The music started, and Simonie began to dance in a counter-clockwise direction around the circle, his feet jigging to the rhythm. Remembering David's words, he relaxed and let his body move the way the music felt.

Simonie's arms flew out from his sides, his elbows bent, and his fingers spread. Feeling as though the music had caused something inside him to take flight, his arms moved like wings as he jigged round and round the circle.

It was not until Simonie heard the quick phrases of the music that signalled the end of his dance that he noticed the crowd whistling and cheering. He and Dana moved off the floor and out of the circle as another pair of dancers took their place.

Simonie was too excited to sit down. He found Anaana and Ataata at the back of the room, where they were watching the dancers.

"You did so well, Simonie!" whispered Anaana, putting an arm around his shoulders. Ataata gave him a thumbs-up.

After what seemed to Simonie like endless other pairs of dancers, it was finally time for the winners to be announced. Simonie held his breath. The emcee called out the third place winners. Simonie clapped and waited anxiously. Then second place. Simonie was so nervous he even forgot to clap.

"And the winners of the first prize," said the emcee, smiling out at the audience, "are Simonie and Dana!"

Simonie looked at Dana and grinned. They raced to the front of the room to collect their prize.

Anaana and Ataata cheered, and Simonie heard David yell, "Hooray!"

After accepting his prize, Simonie moved through the crowd toward Anaana and Ataata, receiving smiles and pats on the back from his friends and their families.

Anaana and Ataata both gave him a big hug when he reached them.

"You learned to feel the music, Simonie!" Ataata said proudly.

"Merry Christmas!" someone in the crowd called. As the call spread through the crowd, and everyone wished their neighbours a merry Christmas, the music started again, and everyone began to dance.

As Simonie danced with his parents, he felt proud and happy. And most importantly, he knew he had danced his best.

ACKNOWLEDGEMENTS

I extend my sincere appreciation and thanks to Kathleen Keenan. Your editorial expertise, knowledge and professionalism guided me throughout the process that led to the fruition of this work. I learned so much as I faced the struggles of learning to write my first children's book. When there were difficult times, I felt always encouraged to keep at it. Thank you for everything you did to support the work and for your generosity and kindness when I was grieving the loss of my only brother, Roger, during this project.

—GAIL MATTHEWS

CONTRIBUTORS

GAIL MATTHEWS lives in Taloyoak, Nunavut, where she teaches English language arts at Netsilik School. She has travelled across Canada's Arctic region and has also worked in Ivujivik, Nunavik. Gail is a teacher educator, researcher, writer, and dancer. She has published research papers on literacy, teacher education, and curriculum. Gail earned her PhD at the University of Toronto and was an assistant professor of literacy at the University of New Brunswick Saint John. She is a graduate of the Teacher Training Program at Canada's National Ballet School and continues to teach children ballet and Israeli folk dance.

ALI HINCH has been working as a full-time illustrator and designer in educational kids' literature since getting her degree in illustration from Sheridan College. She's also dabbled in puppet concepts, set design, storyboarding, and writing for animation. Currently living in Toronto, she spends a lot of time drinking iced tea and making new dog friends.

INHABIT
MEDIA

IQALUIT · TORONTO